the POWERPUFF GIRLS

The SUPER SECRET

SAVING THE DAY Notebook

BY OLIVIA LONDON

An Imprint of Penguin Random House

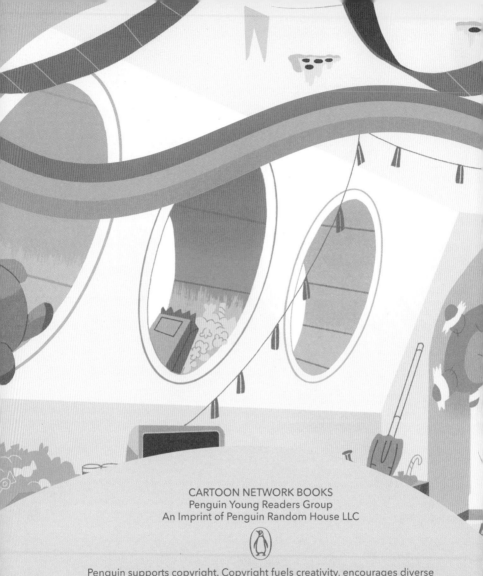

CARTOON NETWORK BOOKS
Penguin Young Readers Group
An Imprint of Penguin Random House LLC

Cover illustration by Derek Charm

TM and © Cartoon Network. (s16). All rights reserved. Published in 2016 by Cartoon Network Books, an imprint of Penguin Random House LLC, 345 Hudson Street, New York, New York 10014. Manufactured in China.

ISBN 9780399541612   10 9 8 7 6 5 4 3 2 1

THIS JOURNAL BELONGS TO:

WELCOME TO TOWNSVILLE!

Wave hello to the Powerpuff Girls!
They are off to keep their quiet, peaceful home
of Townsville safe from the evil supervillains that lurk
in the darkness. No one can keep Townsville safe better
than the Powerpuff Girls! But wait a minute . . . do you see
what I see? Some evil force has wreaked havoc on Townsville,
flattening most of the buildings! Townsville is almost
destroyed, and it's up to you and the Powerpuff Girls
to put it back together again. Draw in the missing
pieces before Townsville is lost . . . FOREVER!

ALL ABOUT BLOSSOM

Ah . . . Blossom! One of our fearless superheroes. But just how well do YOU really know Blossom? Do you know her deepest, most secret thoughts? Do you know how many extra-credit assignments she's done for her teacher? Do you know what kind of spirit animal she has?! It's time to test your knowledge. Fill in the blanks with your best answers!

Blossom's color is _____ .

Blossom gets her powfactor from her _____ ,

_____ , and _____ .

In the trio, is Blossom the *PEACEMAKER*, the

LEADER, or the *INSTIGATOR*? Circle one.

THIS IS WHAT BLOSSOM LOOKS LIKE!

6

Blossom probably dreams about

~~~~~~

~~~~~~

~~~~~~

~~~~~~

Blossom's biggest fear is most likely

~~~~~~

~~~~~~

~~~~~~

~~~~~~

Blossom is best known for being

~~~~~~

~~~~~~

~~~~~~

~~~~~~

ALL ABOUT BUBBLES

Cute, sweet little Bubbles!

Everyone's best friend . . . or is she? How well

do YOU know Bubbles? Do you know what her favorite

stuffed animal is? Do you know what she eats for breakfast?

Do you know what song she sings when she's scared, to

help her be brave? It's time to test your knowledge.

Fill in the blanks with your best answers!

Bubbles's color is ....

Bubbles gets her powfactor from her ....,

......................, and ....

In the trio, is Bubbles the *PEACEMAKER*, the

LEADER, or the *INSTIGATOR*? Circle one.

THIS IS WHAT BUBBLES LOOKS LIKE!

"AFTER I PUNCH YOU OUT, LET'S HUG IT OUT!"
—BUBBLES

Bubbles probably dreams about

....
....
....
....

Bubbles's biggest fear is most likely

....
....
....
....

Bubbles is best known for being

....
....
....
....
....

ALL ABOUT BUTTERCUP

Buttercup, the toughest Powerpuff Girl.
Does she let *anyone* through that rough exterior,
or does she keep everything locked inside like
a vault? Let's find out. How well do YOU know
Buttercup? Do you know her coolest tricks? Do you know
her best Dragon Wizard Skateboard Fighters score?
Do you know if she snores while she sleeps?! It's time to test
your knowledge. Fill in the blanks with your best answers!

Buttercup's color is _____.

Buttercup gets her powfactor from her _____,

_____, and _____.

In the trio, is Buttercup the PEACEMAKER, the

LEADER, or the INSTIGATOR? Circle one.

THIS IS WHAT BUTTERCUP LOOKS LIKE!

Buttercup probably dreams about

Buttercup's biggest fear is most likely

Buttercup is best known for being

Powerpuff Quiz!

1. It's Monday morning, and your homework assignment from over the weekend is due. You:

a. Were going to do it, you swear! But then you started playing Dragon Wizard and you were really kicking butt so you played all night. Then you were going to do it on Sunday but something came up . . . Oh well. Who needs grammar, anyway?!

b. Did it on Friday night, double-checked all the answers on Saturday. And triple-checked them on Sunday, just to be sure. Plus, you did an extra credit assignment that you made up yourself.

c. You did it on Saturday afternoon, like you usually do. And then you went to hang out with some of your friends and didn't look back.

2. You're going to Splash City Water Park with your family, and you can't wait to:

a. Ride the ROCKTOPUS! It's supposed to be the biggest, scariest water roller coaster of all time. No joke.

b. Hit whatever rides everyone else wants to go on! It'll all be fun—you're along for the ride!

c. Check out the backstage tour to see how all the rides work. Isn't science awesome?!

3. There's a dance at your school. You wear:

a. Uh . . . the same outfit you're already wearing? Dances are weird.

b. It's so hard to decide! In fact, you spend hours at home getting ready. You love fashion and beauty, and you have so many favorite outfits that it's really hard to choose. But eventually you find the perfect outfit, of course!

c. Well, based on what you know about school dances, logically you determine that you are supposed to get dressed up. So, naturally, you do what you're supposed to do!

4. It's time to fight the bad guys. Your driving force is:

a. Rage. Pure rage.

b. Friendship and love for the people you care about.

c. Logic and deductive reasoning.

5. Your favorite pastime is:

a. Playing video games or sports. Anything that involves showing the losers who's boss.

b. Something artistic, like coloring or making your own clothes.

c. Organizing your room. Alphabetizing is exhilarating!

6. What do you think you're most likely to be when you grow up?

a. The front woman (or man!) of some covert CIA black ops group.

b. A yoga teacher. Or a makeup artist. Or maybe a fashion designer!

c. The president.

Mostly a's: You're a full-on Buttercup, dude. You love kicking the bad guys' butts, and you're not afraid of, well, anything! You're not so great at following rules, but when something important is at stake, you're always there for the ones you love. You're a bit of a daredevil, and you don't conform to what society thinks you should do. You're strong-willed and your friends really respect you for speaking your mind.

Mostly b's:
You're bursting with peace, love, and friendship—just like Bubbles! You love having fun, and you value friendship above all. You want everyone to just get along, but when push comes to shove, if you have to fight, you fight for the right reasons. You're driven and you follow rules well, but you don't go overboard. You still know how to have fun. Your friends love how balanced and easygoing you are.

Mostly c's: You will rule the world with logic, just like Blossom. You love order and organization, and you always go above and beyond what is asked of you. You love learning and discovering how things work, and you apply those lessons to help you become a terrific leader. You like to have fun just as much as the next guy, but you see the bigger picture and realize that some things are more important than fun. Your friends always come to you for help and advice because they know they can rely on your wisdom.

POWERPUFF PHOTO DOODLE!

Now that you know which Powerpuff Girl you are most like, turn the doodle below into you as that Powerpuff Girl! How? It's easy: Find a photo of yourself that you like, and cut out your face. (Make sure it's big enough to fit in the empty circle on the Powerpuff body drawn below.) Then draw in the rest of your Powerpuff Girl's attributes!

WHERE DO YOU GET _YOUR_ POWFACTOR FROM?

Time to Save the Day!

The Powerpuff Girls are in class at their new school when the phone rings! The city of Townsville needs them, but can they get to the Mayor in time? Help them get from school to the Mayor's office without any delays!

finish

start

BUBBLES'S DIY ART!

Bubbles loves all things pretty and
crafty. That's why she's SUPER into do-it-
yourself projects—like her Beauty Blog (even though
that got totally messed up by Buttercup and Blossom!).
For her latest project, Bubbles wants to personalize her space
in her shared bedroom so it feels cozy and comforting, but,
most of all, totally Bubbles-licious! See? How would you
like to do your own DIY project just like Bubbles?
Awesome!

COLLECT ONE OF EACH OF THE FOLLOWING FOR YOUR OWN MULTIMEDIA ART PROJECT:

1 **3-D object** (This means anything that has at least three
sides, like a toy, a piece of candy, or a barrette. Anything
you can hold in your hand is fair game!)

1 **piece of text** (Pick your favorite quote from a song or
book, or even something that you wrote.)

1 **printed image** (Find any picture, whether it's
a photograph, a page from a magazine, or a poster on
your wall.)

2 **different types of writing utensils**
(You got this one, right?)

Now create your own piece of artwork using each of the listed items. One of the things that makes art AWESOME is that it can be almost anything as long as it has a point of view. You can use these items to make a statement, to create something beautiful, or to express yourself. There is no wrong way to do this project. Seriously, you can tie all your items together and make a necklace; you can paste them all on a T-shirt; you can write a story about how they all connect. You can even add more items to your piece of artwork if you'd like. The most important thing is to have fun!

BLOSSOM'S LISTMANIA!

Our little Blossom is so organized and put together, it's no wonder she's the leader of the Powerpuff Girls! In fact, sometimes she takes her organization a little too far . . . like that time she thought she overslept and was going to be late for school when it was really only Sunday. Still, how does she stay so very organized? Well, she makes lists, of course! Lots and lots of lists. In fact, she was just about to make some lists when she got called away to go fight Man-Boy. Will you finish them for her? Fantastic!

And look! She left in such a hurry that she didn't even have time to name the last two lists. What do YOU think the mystery lists were going to be?

Blossom's Back-to-School List

1. ~~~~~~

2. ~~~~~~

3. ~~~~~~

4. ~~~~~~

5. ~~~~~~

6. ~~~~~~

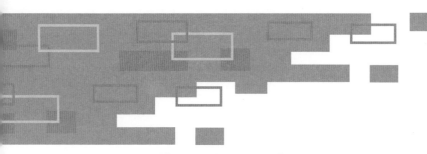

Blossom's To-Do List

1. ~~~~~~

2. ~~~~~~

3. ~~~~~~

4. ~~~~~~

5. ~~~~~~

6. ~~~~~~

Blossom's Favorite Books List

1. ~~~~~~~~~~~~~~~~~~~~~~~~~~~~~~~~

2. ~~~~~~~~~~~~~~~~~~~~~~~~~~~~~~~~~~~~

3. ~~~~~~~~~~~~~~~~~~~~~~~~~~~~

4. ~~~~~~~~~~~~~~~~~~~~~~~~~~~~

5. ~~~~~~~~~~~~~~~~~~~~~~~~~~

6. ~~~~~~~~~~~~~~~~~~~~~~~~~~

Blossom's List of DOs

1. ～～～～～～～～～～～～～～～～～～～～～～
2. ～～～～～～～～～～～～～～～～～～～～～～
3. ～～～～～～～～～～～～～～～～～～～～～～
4. ～～～～～～～～～～～～～～～～～～～～～～
5. ～～～～～～～～～～～～～～～～～～～～～～
6. ～～～～～～～～～～～～～～～～～～～～～～

Blossom's List of DON'Ts

1. ～～～～～～～～～～～～～～～～～～～～～～
2. ～～～～～～～～～～～～～～～～～～～～～～
3. ～～～～～～～～～～～～～～～～～～～～
4. ～～～～～～～～～～～～～～～～～～～～
5. ～～～～～～～～～～～～～～～～～
6. ～～～～～～～～～～～～～～～～～

Blossom's List of Villains

1. _____
2. _____
3. _____
4. _____
5. _____
6. _____

Blossom's List of _____

1. _____ 4. _____
2. _____ 5. _____
3. _____ 6. _____

Blossom's List of _____

1. _____ 4. _____
2. _____ 5. _____
3. _____ 6. _____

Dear Diary, Love, Bubbles

Today was a pretty good day, until Blossom and Buttercup started fighting. I hate it when they fight. It makes me feel totally and completely bummed out. Why can't everyone just get along? Don't they understand how important friendship is? I mean, friendship . . . Well, friendship is the ship atop the friend sea! It's . . . it's totally majestical. Plus, when they fight it makes me feel super sad. Please, please make it stop! I wish all these superpowers we have could make people love each other more . . .

HAVE YOU EVER FELT SAD ABOUT SOMETHING JUST LIKE BUBBLES AND WANTED TO SHARE YOUR FEELINGS? NOW'S YOUR CHANCE! USE THE SPACE BELOW LIKE A JOURNAL AND WRITE ABOUT A TIME YOU FELT SAD AND WHY.

THE BUTTERCUP SCRAMBLE!

Buttercup is one feisty superhero! But even though her anger is helpful when fighting the bad guys, she can sometimes lose her temper when there are no villains in sight. Like that time she couldn't dunk a basket at lunch and got all bent out of shape? Or when she was searching the beach for that last bottle cap for her collection and found a can instead? Sometimes she gets so fiery that she tears things to pieces! Important things . . . like maps and clues. Can you help her piece this torn-up ransom note back together? Townsville and the Powerpuff Girls need you!

SURRENDER

I

HAVE

GIRLS,

ELSE!

THE

OR

KIDNAPPED

POWERPUFF

MAYOR.

DEAR

SINCERELY,
MOJO JOJO

Superpower Me Up Quiz!

IF YOU WERE A SUPERHERO,
WHAT SUPERPOWER WOULD YOU HAVE?
TAKE THIS QUIZ TO FIND OUT!

1. True or False: I am afraid of heights.

a. 100 percent true. Flying? No thank you, I'll walk.

b. Not true, but it's also not my favorite thing.

c. 150 percent false. Bring it on.

2. Did you know that when you cut a worm in half, it grows a new head and tail and becomes two worms? That is so:

a. Gross. Bodies should NOT change like that.

b. Cool, but don't ask *me* to cut it in half!

c. Totally awesome. Can I try?

3. True or False: I wish I could communicate with animals.

a. 100 percent true. That would be amazing!

b. Eh, that would be cool, but what I'd really like to do is make them do what I say!

c. Totally 100 percent false. I don't want to communicate with them—I want to turn into one!

4. How cool would it be to predict the future?

a. Uh, so cool. Like, the coolest thing ever. Then I could stop wasting so much time reading my horoscope!

b. Can I read someone else's mind instead?

c. Make me an invisible fly on the wall of every top secret meeting across the globe and I would predict the future better than any psychic!

5. How many languages would you like to speak?

a. A million, at least.

b. I've never really thought about it.

c. Who cares? Words are lame. Actions are the bomb!

6. If you could clone yourself, would you?

a. No way. It's hard enough keeping tabs on one body, let alone two.

b. Depends. Can I control my clone?

c. Yes! See, that's what I'm talking about! Total physical domination.

Mostly a's: Your superpower is mental-based powers. That means that you would most likely have a power that would somehow enhance your own mental abilities. For example, you might know multiple languages, be able to understand animals and plant life, or be psychic. You're not interested in manipulating anyone but yourself.

Mostly b's:

Your superpower is physical manipulation. You like getting a bit physical, but you'd rather have powers that can affect other people physically than those that will affect your own body. For example, you might be able to move objects with your mind, or have special healing powers, or be able to manipulate the elements like water, air, light, and fire.

Mostly c's: Your superpower is totally physical. That means for you, power is all about the body. YOUR body. You would have powers that affect your own physical abilities, but no one else's. For example, you might be able to become invisible, or shape-shift, or have the power of flight.

TROUBLE PUFFS

Even the Powerpuff Girls make wrong turns sometimes and end up doing things they shouldn't. Like that time when Blossom wanted to impress Dr. Kensington so badly that she accidentally put Townsville in danger. Or when Buttercup wanted the Derbytantes to like her so badly that she abandoned her sisters. Can you think of a time when you made a mistake you wished you hadn't made? Write about that time, how you felt, and if/how you tried to fix what you had done.

POWERPUFF GIRLS CALENDAR

The Powerpuff Girls are always saving the day!
That means they are three very busy little superheroes.
It makes you wonder how they keep all of their
appointments and duties in check *and* how they
remember everything that happens to them day
after day, doesn't it? Well, they use this handy weekly
journal that Blossom created, of course! Do you have
a weekly journal that you write in to keep track of your
week? Try to fill in this journal for one week and see
how much of your life you remember!

Monday

TODAY'S DATE: _____

Today I wore _____

My favorite part of the school day was

_____

_____

_____

_____

because _____

_____

_____

For lunch, I ate _____

This day was special because _____

_____

_____

After school, I _____

_____

I like Mondays because _____

_____

_____

I don't like Mondays because _____

_____

_____

Tonight I read _____

Tuesday

TODAY'S DATE: _____

Today I wore _____

> ## My favorite part of the school day was
>
> _____
>
> _____
>
> _____
>
> _____
>
> because _____
>
> _____
>
> _____

For lunch, I ate _____

This day was special because

After school, I

I like Tuesdays because

I don't like Tuesdays because

Tonight I read

Wednesday

Today I wore _____

My favorite part of the school day was

_____

_____

_____

_____

because _____

_____

_____

For lunch, I ate _____

This day was special because _____

_____

_____

After school, I _____

_____

I like Wednesdays because _____

_____

_____

I don't like Wednesdays because _____

_____

_____

Tonight I read _____

Thursday

TODAY'S DATE: _____

Today I wore _____

My favorite part of the school day was

_____

_____

_____

_____

because _____

_____

_____

For lunch, I ate _____

This day was special because

After school, I

I like Thursdays because

I don't like Thursdays because

Tonight I read

Friday

TODAY'S DATE: _____

Today I wore _____

My favorite part of the school day was

_____

_____

_____

_____

because _____

_____

_____

For lunch, I ate _____

This day was special because _____

_____

_____

After school, I _____

_____

I like Fridays because _____

_____

_____

I don't like Fridays because _____

_____

_____

Tonight I read _____

Saturday

TODAY'S DATE: _____

Today I wore _____

My favorite part of the day was

_____

_____

_____

_____

because _____

_____

_____

For lunch, I ate _____

This day was special because

In the afternoon, I

I like Saturdays because

I don't like Saturdays because

Tonight I read

Sunday

Today I wore _____

My favorite part of the day was

_____

_____

_____

_____

because _____

_____

_____

For lunch, I ate _____

This day was special because _____

_____

_____

In the afternoon, I _____

_____

I like Sundays because _____

_____

_____

I don't like Sundays because _____

_____

_____

Tonight I read _____

Yo Diary, It's Me, Buttercup

S'up, it's Buttercup. I'm totally not into journals, but Bubbles dared me to write in one for a day and you know me—can't say no to a dare! Anyway, today Man-Boy stole all of the water from Townsville. Can you believe it? Man, I really, really hate supervillains. Like, I hate them so much I can literally feel my blood boiling. I wish we could lock them all up in Albatross Prison FOREVER and EVER. But instead they are just out there, living their lives like the rest of us. It makes me so mad I could . . . I could just . . . Wait a minute! What am I doing sitting here writing in some girly journal when I should be out there kicking some major bad-guy butt???? Gotta run.

HAVE YOU EVER BEEN REALLY, REALLY ANGRY ABOUT SOMETHING SOMEONE DID TO YOU AND WANTED TO SHARE YOUR FEELINGS? NOW'S YOUR CHANCE! USE THE SPACE BELOW LIKE A JOURNAL AND WRITE ABOUT A TIME YOU WERE ANGRY AND WHY.

BLOSSOM'S VILLAIN SEARCH!

Everyone knows that Townsville has its fair share of supervillains. No one keeps better track of them than Blossom. She keeps tabs and lists on everyone and everything! It's in her blood. But something's happened to her top secret list of villains (okay . . . Buttercup smashed a bug with it and then flushed it down the toilet, but don't tell Blossom!) and she needs your help re-creating it. Can you find all of the villains that are a threat to Townsville in the word search?

MOJO JOJO

HIM

MORBUCKS

PACK RAT

BIANCA BIKINI

BARBARUS BIKINI

MAN-BOY

ALLEGRO

SILICO

FUZZY LUMPKINS

```
B K G R P W M M Z H Z A W B D
E A H P D E Y R Y I M F P I I
Y K R I M Q O T W T A C A A N
B C J B M O B T A Z N K C N X
I Q L W A C J P Q P B Y K C X
O R I F P R E O V U O E R A P
M B P F T M U A J R Y N A B A
O M A W F G M S B O B D T I C
R M L D B Q P R B U J W V K X
B Z L Y W G A A P I U O C I S
U E E H X K O A A T K B T N I
C B G G W E C U X O P I I I L
K M R F Q W I O G U K A N R I
S I O C O A G Z Y M F M F I C
F U Z Z Y L U M P K I N S Y O
```

Mix It Up!

Bubbles, Blossom, and Buttercup are a team, but they aren't all alike, that's for sure! Each Powerpuff Girl has her own unique personality, from her hairstyle to her superpowers to the kind of music she loves to listen to. It looks like the girls were spending their downtime making music mixes when they got called away to save Townsville from the evil Pack Rat!

Do you think YOU know each Powerpuff Girl well enough to fill in the mixes she started? Okay then, go for it! Then make up a brand-new mix of your very own!

BLOSSOM'S SUPER STUDY-UP MIX

1. ⁓⁓⁓⁓⁓⁓⁓⁓⁓⁓⁓⁓⁓⁓⁓⁓⁓
2. ⁓⁓⁓⁓⁓⁓⁓⁓⁓⁓⁓⁓⁓⁓⁓⁓⁓
3. ⁓⁓⁓⁓⁓⁓⁓⁓⁓⁓⁓⁓⁓⁓⁓⁓⁓
4. ⁓⁓⁓⁓⁓⁓⁓⁓⁓⁓⁓⁓⁓⁓⁓⁓⁓
5. ⁓⁓⁓⁓⁓⁓⁓⁓⁓⁓⁓⁓⁓⁓⁓⁓⁓

6. ⁓⁓⁓⁓⁓⁓⁓⁓⁓⁓⁓⁓⁓⁓⁓⁓⁓
7. ⁓⁓⁓⁓⁓⁓⁓⁓⁓⁓⁓⁓⁓⁓⁓⁓⁓
8. ⁓⁓⁓⁓⁓⁓⁓⁓⁓⁓⁓⁓⁓⁓⁓⁓⁓
9. ⁓⁓⁓⁓⁓⁓⁓⁓⁓⁓⁓⁓⁓⁓⁓⁓⁓
10. ⁓⁓⁓⁓⁓⁓⁓⁓⁓⁓⁓⁓⁓⁓⁓⁓⁓

BUTTERCUP'S SAVE-THE-DAY MIX

1. _____
2. _____
3. _____
4. _____
5. _____

6. _____
7. _____
8. _____
9. _____
10. _____

1. .... 6. ....
2. .... 7. ....
3. .... 8. ....
4. .... 9. ....
5. .... 10. ....

BUBBLES'S CODE-CRACKING MIX

1. .... 6. ....
2. .... 7. ....
3. .... 8. ....
4. .... 9. ....
5. .... 10. ....

MY _____ MIX

ONCE UPON A TOWNSVILLE...

Townsville has survived so many crazy events and scary villains who have threatened to destroy it. Like the time it was taken over by a powerful rainbow that hypnotized everyone into being happy about everything all the time—even car accidents! Or the time Professor Utonium's Transmogrifying Ray turned Donny into a giant monster that began tearing up the town!

NOW IT'S YOUR TURN TO WRITE YOUR OWN STORY ABOUT TOWNSVILLE AND THE POWERPUFF GIRLS SAVING THE DAY!

Double Take!

Have you ever wanted to be a crime-fighting superhero just like the Powerpuff Girls? Well, fighting crime and solving mysteries takes some very important skills. One of the most important skills is being able to observe a scene and pick out seemingly small but vital details and clues. Try out this test to see if you have what it takes to fight crime! Below are two almost identical pictures of Townsville—except for TWELVE minor differences.

Can you find them?

MY FAVORITE ADVENTURES SCRAPBOOK!

The Powerpuff Girls aren't just sisters, they're best friends. They love going through old scrapbooks of their adventures together—and boy, have they had a lot of them! Do you have a best friend who you share your adventures with? Now you can put together your own special keepsake scrapbook of your adventures with your best friend! Look through your pictures and choose the ones that best describe the adventures listed below. If your pictures are mostly digital, print the pictures you choose.

NOW PASTE THOSE PICTURES INTO THE SCRAPBOOK! YOU CAN EVEN FILL IN YOUR OWN ADVENTURES, AND DRAW A PICTURE OF YOU AND YOUR BESTIE FIVE YEARS FROM NOW. HAPPY SCRAPBOOKING!

OUR MOST FUN ADVENTURE

OUR SCARIEST ADVENTURE

OUR SILLIEST ADVENTURE

OUR MOST SPECIAL ADVENTURE

OUR FAVORITE PLACE

OUR .... ADVENTURE

OUR TOWN

ME AND . . . . AS BABIES

ME AND . . . . AT HALLOWEEN

ME AND .... NOW

ME AND .... IN FIVE YEARS!

Powerpuff Fashion Sense!

WHAT'S YOUR INNER POWERPUFF GIRL FASHION SENSE?
ARE YOU LIKE BUTTERCUP, BUBBLES, OR BLOSSOM? TAKE THIS QUIZ AND FIND OUT!

1. It's the first day of school. You:

a. Wear the perfect outfit you picked out months ago, duh! Jeans, a button-down blouse, and a matching cardigan with adorable ballet flats. Done and done.

b. Spend the weekend rifling through the trendiest new fashion mags and going in and out of boutiques until you finally come across this one-of-a-kind, totally adorable outfit that says I'm super down-to-earth, but I have major style.

c. Uh, wear jeans and a T-shirt?

2. You're invited to a pool party. You:

a. Wear the black-and-white one-piece you got last summer. It's only a year old, plus it's way better than a two-piece for playing water sports.

b. Wear the adorable aqua polka-dot bikini with the lace fringe. Who cares if it's not ideal for roughhousing, it's so cute!

c. Throw on the bathing suit you used to wear when you were on the swim team and call it a day. Oh, and you pack your goggles for laps.

3. Your favorite finds are:

a. Matching, put together for you, or on sale!

b. Creative, unique, and crafty

c. T-shirts with awesome band names or video-game characters on them

4. Your favorite colors are:

a. Red, orange, and pink

b. Blue, yellow, and white

c. Green, black, and teal

5. You wear dresses because:

a. You're going to something dressy, and you always dress to impress!

b. You love being adorable and chic.

c. Someone is forcing you to.

6. If you were designing your own shirt, you would:

a. Make it perfectly symmetrical.

b. Make it transform into a dress to wear out at night!

c. Add lots of storage for snacks.

Mostly a's: Your fashion sense is like Blossom's. Logical, practical, and always proper! You like matching outfits and sets you can purchase together so you know it will look good but you won't have to do a whole lot of creative thinking. While fashion may not be your favorite thing, you're always dressed to impress, and you never wear the wrong thing to the wrong place.

Mostly b's: You're Bubbles, aka the Fashion Guru of the Powerpuff Girls. You love fashion and beauty, and you're always looking for a new, fresh take on something old or classic. You're not afraid to take risks with your wardrobe, and truth be told, you like throwing yourself into it and getting creative. People admire your ability to make fashion work for you!

Mostly c's: You probably guessed it already, but you're 100 percent Buttercup. You don't care about fashion or what people think of you—you're too busy kicking some bad-guy butt. You're perfectly fine with a soft T-shirt and a comfortable pair of jeans, and you know what? That's just fine, because people love you for your smarts and sparkling personality—not your closet.

CHANNELING YOUR POWFACTOR!

The Powerpuff Girls have dedicated their lives to fighting crime and keeping Townsville safe. They're superheroes, after all! But you don't have to be a superhero to know right from wrong . . . right? Were there times in your life when you were asked to make a choice to do the right thing or to help someone in need, just like the Powerpuff Girls do every day? Use the prompts to help you remember the times when you were a Powerpuff Girl in your own life!

I was really proud of myself because

. . . .

. . . .

. . . .

. . . .

. . . .

. . . .

. . . .

I came to a friend's rescue when I

....

....

....

....

....

....

....

I feel powerful because I am

....

....

....

....

I made the right decision when I

I am the strongest when

....

....

....

....

....

....

....

....

I think powfactor means

....

....

....

....

....

....

....

....

My best attribute is

....

....

....

....

....

....

....

....

If I saw someone doing something wrong, I would

....

....

....

....

....

....

....

....

....

Dear Diary, Love, Blossom

Today was an amazing day! I spent it in the lab with the Professor doing really important science research, and I actually made a discovery! That's right. I helped the Professor figure out how to reprogram his Transmogrifying Ray. But after a whole day of testing it and retesting it and programming and reprogramming, I realized that there was a glitch in the Professor's mathematical equation. He was so happy he high-fived me and called me his little lab partner! I'm so excited I could scream. But I won't. Anyway, I don't think I've ever been this proud of myself in my whole life!!! High five, me!

HAVE YOU EVER BEEN SO SUPERPROUD OF YOURSELF THAT YOU WANTED TO WRITE ALL ABOUT IT? NOW'S YOUR CHANCE! USE THE SPACE BELOW LIKE A JOURNAL AND WRITE ABOUT A TIME YOU WERE PROUD AND WHY.

POWERPUFF YOURSELF!

Do you love the Powerpuff Girls so much that you want to BE one? If you could create a Powerpuff Girl identity for yourself, what would it be? Would her personality be just like yours? What would your color be? How would you wear your hair? What's your personal style? Use the space below to draw your very own Powerpuff Girl now!

NOW DRAW YOUR NEW POWERPUFF GIRL

FIGHTING ONE OF YOUR BIGGEST, TOUGHEST ENEMIES!

start

Not So Fast, Mojo Jojo!

Oh no! Mojo Jojo has created a new cybermonster that's set to destroy Townsville! The Powerpuff Girls are on their way, but it's a long trip from where they are to Mojo. Can you get them to their destination as quickly as possible? Hurry up before Townsville is lost forever!

finish

Powerpuff Girls to the Rescue!

Blossom, Buttercup, and Bubbles are always coming to someone's rescue. Usually it's the Mayor. Sometimes it's Professor Utonium. Occasionally it's each other! Ahem, let's not forget about that time they got charmed by their so-called cool new classmate Jemmica and ended up being brainwashed into doing her evil bidding. But through all of these drama bombs, one thing's clear: The Powerpuff Girls ROCK! And, since the Powerpuff Girls are totally awesome, supes rare superheroes, they deserve their very own supercomic.

Use the panels to plot out your very own Powerpuff Girls comic book battle scene! The Powerpuff Girls have just arrived at the scene where the bad buys are trying to destroy Townsville—and the girls are ready to kick some wimpy butt. The phrases below may help you along—use them if you'd like.

"ARE YOU WITH ME?"

"NOBODY MESSES WITH MY SISTERS!"

"I'VE BEEN DUPED!"

"THAT WAS, UM, UNEXPECTED."

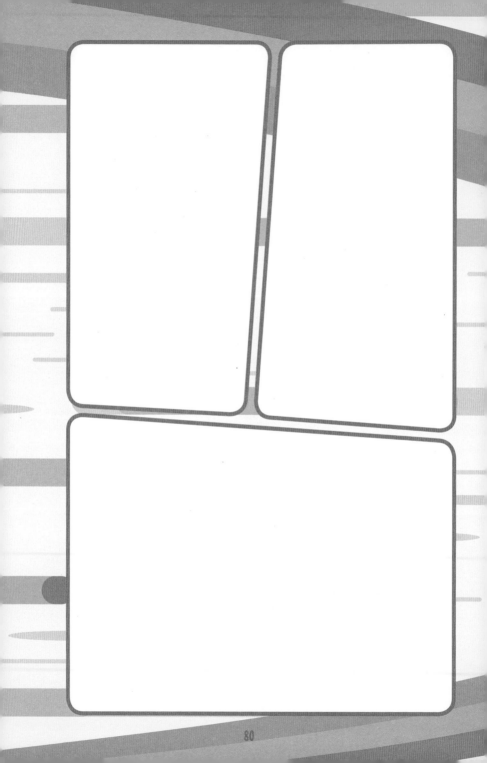

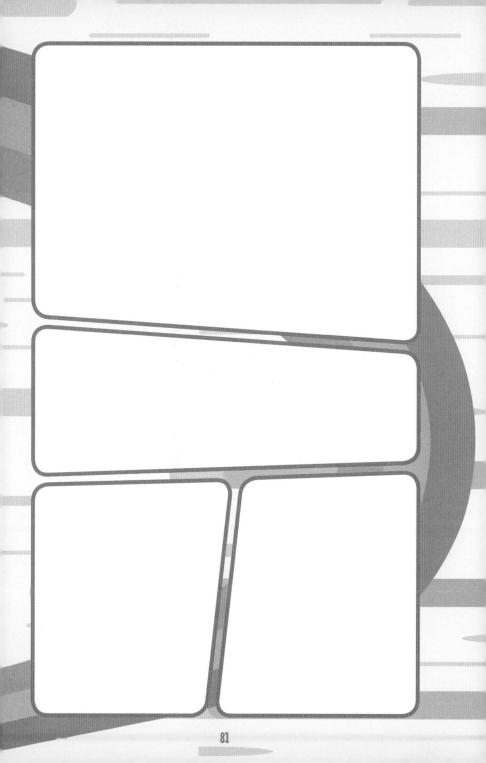

BUTTERCUP'S WORKSHOP!

Buttercup loves coming up with totally awesome
ways to make her life a den of chillaxitude. For
Monster Movie Night with the Professor, she devises
an elaborate snack-fetching contraption to keep them
fully stocked in popcorn and candy without having to
get up from the couch once! After all, she could never
be the Professor's Little Monster Masher if she missed
half the movie going back and forth to the kitchen! Then,
one time, when she was home babysitting her sick sisters,
she made a giant straw out of a bunch of regular straws
that stretched from the soda bottles in the kitchen all the
way into the living room, so all she had to do was lay back
and slurp. Ah, the good life!

Want to make your life into a den of chillaxitude, too?
Think about a task you hate doing, like folding your
clothes, cleaning your room, or brushing your teeth,
and devise your own invention to help you do it
without moving a muscle! Draw the blueprints for
your design here. It's time to trademark!

DECODING 101 WITH BUBBLES!

Oh no! Mojo Jojo has rigged an explosion in the Mayor's office—if the Powerpuff Girls can't decode his secret password and enter it into the machine's keypad in thirty seconds, the office will fill up from top to bottom with a sticky, slimy green sludge! It's a good thing Bubbles loves solving puzzles and is a natural hacker! Can you help her decode the password? Using the decryption key below, you'll find that each letter in the actual alphabet (bottom row) aligns with a letter in the encrypted alphabet (top row). For example, the encrypted letter D is actually a B. Ready? Get cracking!

ENCRYPTED	C	D	E	F	G	H
ACTUAL	A	B	C	D	E	F

I	J	K	L	M	N	O	P	Q	R
G	H	I	J	K	L	M	N	O	P

S	T	U	V	W	X	Y	Z	A	B
Q	R	S	T	U	V	W	X	Y	Z

Here's the encrypted code you need to crack:

OQLQ LQLQ YKNN TWNG VJG YQTNF

UQ NQPI, RRI!

THE STAYOVER SLEEPOVERS

Gathering all your friends for an evening of movie-watching, best-friend talk, and staying up till the sun rises is the absolute rockingest way to spend the night. And nobody loves sleepovers more than the Powerpuff Girls. They love them SO much that every slumber party they've had has been bigger, better, and crazier than the last! Like that one slumber party (you know the one, right?) when they ate WAY too much candy, woke up with crazy sugar headaches, and had no idea what happened to Bubbles?! Thankfully there just happened to be a bull in their kitchen making them breakfast (yum!), because boy, did they need some protein to make it through the rest of that day.

But enough about that, now it's your turn to throw the coolest, most awesome Powerpuff Girl sleepover ever! Which Powerpuff party are YOU going to throw? Start planning now!

Sleepover to-Do Checklist:

_____ Choose a date

_____ Choose a theme

_____ Write out your guest list

_____ Create/write/send your invitations

_____ Buy the decorations/party goods/food

_____ Plan activities and schedule for evening

My Sleepover Party Guest List:

1. ....
2. ....
3. ....
4. ....
5. ....
6. ....
7. ....
8. ....
9. ....
10. ....

BUBBLES'S SLEEPOVER: GAME NIGHT!

DESIGN YOUR GAME-NIGHT INVITATION!

Try to think of something game-themed to include in the design, like a pair of dice, a computer, or a video-game controller.

CREATE YOUR MENU:

Drinks:	Snacks:	Dinner:	Dessert:
1.	1.	1.	1.
2.	2.	2.	2.
3.	3.	3.	3.
4.	4.	4.	4.

MUST-HAVES:

What can't this party do without? Make sure to write it down here so you won't forget it!

1.
2.
3.
4.
5.

DO YOU LOVE DECODING THINGS AND PLAYING GAMES, JUST LIKE BUBBLES? YOU DO?!?! THEN GET READY TO THROW YOUR VERY OWN GAME-NIGHT SLEEPOVER!

List of Game-Related Movie Choices:

Choose three movies that all involve your sleepover theme: games. The word *game* can be in the title, the characters can play a game in the movie, or the whole movie can be like one big mystery game! Get all three movies and let your party guests vote on which one they want to see most!

1. .... 2. .... 3. ....

BEST GAMES TO PLAY: Choose a few games that are awesome for groups. Some games, like scavenger hunts and murder mysteries, take time to plan ahead but can make your party so much fun! Make a list to help decide the schedule for your night.

My Game-Night Party Music Playlist:

Choose as many songs as you can find that use the word *game* in the lyrics and line them up for the ultimate Game Night background music!

1. .... 6. ....
2. .... 7. ....
3. .... 8. ....
4. .... 9. ....
5. .... 10. ....

1. ....
2. ....
3. ....
4. ....
5. ....

BUTTERCUP SLEEPOVER: TREASURE-HUNT ADVENTURE!

DESIGN YOUR TREASURE-HUNT INVITATION!

Try to think of something pirate-y to
include in the design, like a hook, an
eye patch, or a treasure map!

CREATE YOUR MENU:

Drinks:	Snacks:	Dinner:	Dessert:
1.	1.	1.	1.
2.	2.	2.	2.
3.	3.	3.	3.
4.	4.	4.	4.

MUST-HAVES:

What can't this
party do without?
Make sure to write
it down here so you
won't forget it!

1.
2.
3.
4.
5.

ARE YOU ALWAYS ON THE HUNT FOR TROUBLE—WHOOPS!—TREASURE, JUST LIKE BUTTERCUP? YOU ARE?! THEN GET READY TO THROW YOUR VERY OWN TREASURE HUNT ADVENTURE SLEEPOVER!

List of Treasure-Hunt-Related Movie Choices:

Choose three movies that all involve your sleepover theme: treasure hunt! The words *treasure hunt* can be in the title, the characters can go on a treasure hunt in the movie, or maybe they just say the words once! Get all three movies and let your party guests vote on which one they want to see most!

1. _____ 2. _____ 3. _____

BEST GAMES TO PLAY: Choose a few games that are awesome for groups and go with your theme: treasure hunt! You can plan a scavenger hunt or do some funny fill-in-the-blank stories about being lost on a desert island! Make a list to help decide the schedule for your night.

My Treasure-Hunt Party Music Playlist:

Choose as many songs as you can find that use the words *treasure* or *hunt* in the lyrics and line them up for the ultimate Treasure Hunt Sleepover background music!

1. _____ 6. _____
2. _____ 7. _____
3. _____ 8. _____
4. _____ 9. _____
5. _____ 10. _____

1. _____
2. _____
3. _____
4. _____
5. _____

BLOSSOM'S SLEEPOVER: FAVORITE FAIRY TALES!

DESIGN YOUR FAVORITE FAIRY TALES INVITATION!

Try to think of something fairy-tale-
related to include in your design, like a
glass slipper, a spell book, or a wand!

CREATE YOUR MENU:

Drinks:	Snacks:	Dinner:	Dessert:
1.	1.	1.	1.
2.	2.	2.	2.
3.	3.	3.	3.
4.	4.	4.	4.

MUST-HAVES:

What can't this party
do without? Make
sure to write it down
here so you won't
forget it!

1.
2.
3.
4.
5.

List of Fairy-Tale-Related Movie Choices:

Choose three movies that all involve your sleepover theme: fairy tales! The words *fairy tale* can be in the title, the characters can read a fairy tale in the movie, or the whole movie can be like one big fairy tale! Get all three movies and let your party guests vote on which one they want to see most!

1. _____ 2. _____ 3. _____

BEST GAMES TO PLAY: Choose some games that are awesome for groups. Some games, like scavenger hunts and mysteries, take time to plan ahead but can make your party so much fun! You can also reenact your favorite fairy tales by putting on your very own plays! Make a list to help decide the schedule for your night.

1. _____
2. _____
3. _____
4. _____
5. _____

My Favorite Fairy Tale
Party Music Playlist:

Choose as many songs as you can find that use the words *favorite* or *fairy tale* in the lyrics and line them up for the ultimate Favorite Fairy Tale Sleepover background music!

1. _____   6. _____
2. _____   7. _____
3. _____   8. _____
4. _____   9. _____
5. _____ 10. _____

THE MISSING BUNNY SLIPPERS

Quick! The Powerpuff Girls need your help—and so does Townsville! During a sleepover, the girls get so carried away with the slumber party that they don't realize one dangerous detail: Blossom's bunny slippers have been cursed! And what's worse? Now they're MISSING!!! Can you find the cursed bunny slippers before they possess whoever wears them and destroy Townsville?

Blossom's Townsville Checklist

The day is saved! Yet again, thanks to the Powerpuff Girls, the peaceful town of Townsville is safe. But no matter how many times Bubbles and Buttercup reassure Blossom that all is well, she needs to double-check her trusty list of Townsville residents before closing this rescue case. Can you find all of the residents in this word search so Blossom can rest easy, kick her feet up, and play some Dragon Wizard Skateboard Fighters with her sisters?

PROFESSOR

MAYOR

DONNY

MS. KEANE

JARED SHAPIRO

DERBYTANTES

MS. BELLUM

```
M K Q E I Z Y L K D O Q V Y R
D S S C P I B P T D X R V B M
J E B I I N C V G F B V P Y D
X A R E Z R O S D M Q Y R B S
I C R B L K Q C D L D Q O K D
M L O E Y L I M O D Y P F R R
K A A O D T U J N W V T E X Z
Q X Y N B S A M N Q A F S U H
M G A O M N H N Y F Q C S Q J
Z S M H R X I A T N D I O O A
U A K U M J Y K P E S N R S Q
N L Q E R H C R X I S Q E K F
O A H Z A I P V P O R R I F K
U U A E F N X J N X T O Z T V
E L D Z S P E J P K I X X V E
```

Sick Day!

When Blossom and Bubbles get spotted-piglet fever, their snorting, sneezing, red spots, and imaginary thoughts about climbing Mount Everest force them to stay home from school. But when the Professor remembers he has a very important job interview and can't stay home with them, he leaves Buttercup in charge of the sickies! Unfortunately, Buttercup's idea of being *super responsible* includes stuffing her face with barbecue chips and candy, watching her favorite daytime TV show, *Judge Trudy*, and playing lots and lots of video games.

What do you think would happen if Buttercup and Bubbles got sick and Blossom was in charge of nursing them back to health?

Now, what would happen if Buttercup and Blossom got sick and Bubbles had to take care of them?

Which caretaker sister would YOU rather be like, and why?

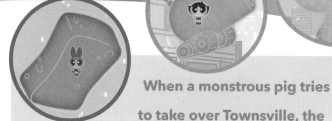

Aura Power!

When a monstrous pig tries
to take over Townsville, the
Powerpuff Girls arrive on the scene
and discover they've just earned some totally
awesome new powers: auras. Their auras
generally take on the shapes and qualities
of things that show off each girl's distinct
personality. Bubbles's auras are usually animals
like giraffes, bunnies, and even piglets, because
she's so sweet and caring, and she LOVES animals.
Remember that time she found a little monster in
the park and wanted to raise it as her own? Well,
that time things didn't go so well . . . How about
the time at the zoo when she found Donny the
Pony and wanted to help him become a unicorn?
Hmmm, okay, that didn't go so well at first, either.
But he did end up being a member of the Unicorn
Coalition Alliance Brigade, so it all worked out!

WHAT DO YOU THINK YOUR AURAS WOULD LOOK LIKE IF YOU HAD POWERS LIKE THE POWERPUFF GIRLS? DRAW SOME OF THEM HERE!

BUTTERCUP'S VILLAIN MASH-UP!

There's nothing Buttercup loves more than beating evil villains until they cry for mercy. If Buttercup isn't kicking some wimpy butt, she might as well not even be awake! The only possible thing that's cooler than an evil villain smackdown is an evil villain *mash-up* smackdown! Create your very own supervillain hybrid mash-ups by matching one villain's head with another's body. Draw your mash-ups in the space provided. Then name your new hybrid villains.

Ready. Set. SMACKDOWN!

SNOWED IN!

After a snow day saves
Blossom from being asked out by a
boy (yikes!) at school, she realizes that if she
can just keep the snow coming with her superpower
ice breath, she might never have to face up to
reality. But will Townsville survive eternal
winter?

DOODLE IN YOUR VERSION OF TOWNSVILLE COVERED WITH SNOW, THANKS TO
BLOSSOM'S COLD FRONT. ADD THE POWERPUFF GIRLS INTO THE SCENE, TOO!

The Powerpuff Girls' TOP TEN Tips for Saving the Day!

Okay . . . So Blossom did have a list of the TOP TEN TIPS FOR SAVING THE DAY but it looks like Bubbles doodled all over it when she was trying to come up with story ideas for her Beauty Blog. Whoops! Can you re-create Blossom's list? (Here's a hint: If you were a Powerpuff Girl, what would your tips be?)

add bows!

new hats for Octi!

1.

2.

3.

4.

5.

6.

7.

8.

9.

10.

Answer Key

**DEAR POWERPUFF GIRLS,
I HAVE KIDNAPPED THE MAYOR.
SURRENDER OR ELSE!**

Page 49

Pages 56–57

Pages 76–77

Pages 94–95

Page 97

111

Congratulations! You're a bona fide Powerpuff Girl now.

Remember when you Powerpuffed yourself earlier on?

Draw the Powerpuff version of yourself into the group!

Don't forget to give yourself a special quote.

The day is saved. The end!